THEFT IN THE RAIN

William Heyliger

first published in

1935

Joe Morrow, very sleepy, grew conscious of voices coming up from the porch—the slow drawl of his uncle, Dr. David Stone, and a quicker, sharper voice. Abruptly the sharper tone scratched at his memory and the drowsiness was gone. What was Harley Kent doing here? So far as he knew the man had never visited the house before, and his uncle had never set foot on the Kent place a quarter of a mile down the road. A word, stark and clear, came through the bedroom window. Robbery! And suddenly he was out of bed and slipping into his clothes.

The morning was cool and fresh after the heavy rain of the

night. His uncle stood at the porch railing, sightless eyes turned off across the valley, a great, tawny German shepherd dog at his side. Harley Kent crowded the top step, and Joe noticed that the dog sneezed, and grew restless, and drew back a step.

"Lady, easy." Dr. Stone's hand felt for the dog's head and

rubbed a twitching ear. "When did you say it was discovered, Kent?"

"A little after six o'clock this morning. The maid found a window open and called me. The wall safe was open, too, and the necklace was gone. Could I trouble you for a match, Doctor? I've lost my lighter."

The man stepped upon the porch, and the dog sneezed again and retreated. Dr. Stone brought forth matches, and Harley Kent had to come close to get them. Joe was vaguely conscious that his uncle's face had become intent.

Harley Kent lit a cigar. "I'm not in the habit of keeping

jewels in the house. Mrs. Kent's been in Europe; her ship docks next Monday. We're to attend a dinner that night, and I knew she'd want the necklace. I took it out of a safe deposit box a week ago and brought it home."

Dr. Stone asked a question. "Insured, of course?" "Certainly. Twenty-five thousand."

The boy sucked in his breath and wondered what twenty-five thousand dollars would look like piled up in shining half dollars. The Kent automobile gleamed in front of the house, and a uniformed chauffeur sat motionless behind the wheel.

"You've notified the

police?"

"I tried to, but the storm last night crippled our telephone line. I came over to use yours."

"Ours is out, too."

Harley Kent made an impatient gesture. "That means I'll have to run into the village." The cigar came out of his mouth. "It was an inside job, Doctor. Whoever robbed that safe knew how to get into it. It was opened by combination."

Dr. Stone said coolly, "That's putting it on your own doorstep."

Harley Kent shrugged. "Figure it out for yourself. There were only three of us in the house—Donovan, the chauffeur, the maid, and myself.

Two days ago I forgot to take some papers to New York. I telephoned Donovan to bring them in. They were in the safe and I had to give him the combination. Well, I'm off for the village. I understand you were a police surgeon before——" The man coughed.

"Yes," said Dr. Stone without emotion.

"Before I lost my sight."

"Well, if you'd like to run over and get the feel of a case again——"

"It might be interesting," the doctor said slowly.

Harley Kent went down the steps, a door slammed, and the car rolled away. Joe had a glimpse of the uniformed figure at the wheel, and spoke in a hoarse whisper:

"Will Donovan be put in jail, Uncle David?"

"Perhaps." The hand came up from the dog's head and tapped the porch railing thoughtfully. "What time is it, Joe? About eight?"

"Five after."

"Two hours," Dr. Stone said as though speaking to himself. Abruptly he jerked his head. "Time we had breakfast," he added, and boy and dog followed at his heels. Here, in the home of his widowed sister that had sheltered him for five years, he knew his way perfectly, and there was nothing to mark him out as blind as he walked boldly toward the dining room. And yet at the last moment, his handicap touched him with uncertainty. He had to put out his hand to make sure of the table and then fumble for his chair.

Joe wondered about jails, and was sorry for Donovan. Twice the man had picked him up on the road and carried him into the village, and once he had spent a fascinating afternoon in the Kent garage holding tools while the chauffeur worked on the car. Did they lock a prisoner in a cell and keep him there night and day?

His mother's voice cut through his thoughts. "You're going over, David?"

"I have a reason for wanting to go," the man said.

Joe's heart throbbed. A reason for going. His throat was husky again. "Right away, Uncle David? A policeman has to get there while the trail is hot, doesn't he?"

"There are some trails," Dr. Stone said in his slow drawl, "that do not grow cold."

Out on the porch
he filled a pipe and
smoked quietly. Joe,
watching that lion
head topped by crisp,
unruly white hair,
wondered if his uncle
ever became excited.
He fidgeted and
watched a clock; and
by and by Dr. Stone
knocked the ashes
from his pipe, stood
up, and took a dog's

harness down from a nail.

The dog stretched its great body and held out its head. A stiff leash rose from either side of the harness and joined a wide, hard handle-grip at the top.

"Lady, forward!"

Slowly, protectingly, the massive animal took Dr. Stone down the steps and along the concrete walk to the road.

"Lady, right."

Without hesitation the dog turned right, the tawny body pressed almost against the man's left leg. They were off now, and Dr. Stone's body bent slightly from the waist toward the dog, while his right hand

lightly swung a cane.
He might have been
gifted with sight, so
rapidly did he walk,
so complete was
his confidence in his
four-footed guide. Joe
had to stretch his legs
to keep up with them.
They went past fields
and orchards, fences
and tangles of wild
grape. The doctor's
cane, swinging along,
came in contact at
last, with a wall of

hedge.

"Kent's place, Joe?"

"Yes, sir." Joe's throat throbbed with a twitching pulse.

A telephone repair truck was in the driveway. The dog slowed, and swung aside, pulling on the leash and changing his course. Without hesitation Dr. Stone followed the pull, and the dog led him around and past the truck. They appeared, in their movements, to be one.

The boy said: "I like to watch him do that."

"He's my eyes, Joe. Kent's car?"

"No, sir; a telephone truck. I don't see his car."

"Not back yet," said the doctor, and

whistled soundlessly. They roamed the grounds. The dog at a rapid pace, took the man along one side of the house and deftly manoeuvered him around every tree and bush. In the rear a maid hung a sodden garment on the line and, after a frightened glance at them, disappeared into the house. The wind blew across the valley and the wet sleeve of a coat fluttered and swung toward Dr. Stone's face. He reached out a groping hand, and found the sleeve, and brought it close to his sightless eyes as though trying to pierce a veil of darkness and make out the pattern. Bees droned through a blooming lilac and they moved around to the other side of the house.

"Joe, is there a pine tree on the place?"

Pin pricks ran along the boy's spine. His uncle had never been here before—how did he know about the tree? "Yes, sir."

"A large tree, heavy-branched?"

"Yes, sir."

"Take me there. Lady, forward."

The cane explored the trunk and then slowly tapped the ground.

"About six feet from the house, Joe?"

Joe blinked. "How do you know?"

"Sound echoes," Dr. Stone chuckled. Automobile tires ground the gravel of the driveway.

"It's Mr. Kent," said the boy.

Harley Kent hurried up to them. "Is this village supposed to have a police force?" he demanded. "Had to wait half an hour for Captain Tucker to stroll back from breakfast. There could be a dozen murders committed——" He broke off. "Just a moment, Doctor, and I'll be with you. It occurs to me I may have left that lighter in another suit——"

"The maid hung one out to dry," Dr. Stone said.

"Why, yes." Harley Kent stopped short. "That's it," he added, and was gone. Presently he was back. "Not there. I suppose it will turn up some place. Well, come in; come in. The police should be here before long."

They mounted to the porch and Lady, after the manner of her breed when trained to work with the blind, stopped with her head directly under the knob of the strange door.

"A remarkable animal," Harley Kent

said in admiration. "Well, here's where the job was done, Doctor."

Joe was conscious of strange tremors. Lady, alert, cocked her head and sniffed the air with an inquiring nose. The doctor, halting in the arched doorway leading from the hall, seemed to lose himself in thought.

"There's a door to the left of this room, Kent?"

"Yes; it leads into the dining room."

"And windows in the wall facing this way. They're open now."

Harley Kent gave a startled grunt. "Doctor, if I didn't know you were blind——"

"Air currents," Dr.

Stone said laconically. "I feel them on my face. You feel them, too, but they go unnoticed. You rely on your eyes. The wall safe, then, should be in the solid wall on the right. Correct, Kent?"

"I don't understand it," Harley Kent said, still startled.

The doctor asked an abrupt question. "How

high is that safe from the floor?"

"Six feet, eight inches."

"To work the combination without straining a short man would have to stand upon a chair."

"Exactly, Doctor. None of the chairs was disturbed; none of the cushions trampled. I checked that with the maid."

Dr. Stone's face was impassive. "I gather that means something to you?"

"What would it mean to you if I told you Donovan was a tall man?"

The doctor's sightless eyes were fixed straight ahead as though he saw something that was denied to other men. "Does Donovan know he's suspected?"

"He isn't quite a fool."

A man passed quickly through the hall. Donovan! Joe instinctively stepped closer to the dog. And suddenly, under his feet, the floor boards creaked with a loud, harsh, dry protest.

"Loose boards all over the room," Harley Kent explained. "I never bothered to have them nailed down. With the safe in this room I looked upon them as a burglar alarm. And yet, in the uproar of last night's storm, a cannon ball might have been rolled across the floor and nobody upstairs would have heard it."

His hands made a resigned gesture of defeat. "No matter how sound you think your plans are, you can never be sure."

"No," Dr. Stone said slowly, "there's always a slip."

The telephone truck was gone, and now another car came up the driveway and stopped with a squeal of brakes.

"Captain Tucker has evidently finished his breakfast at last," Harley Kent said with bitter sarcasm. "He'll want to question Donovan. If you don't mind, Doctor——"

"Of course." The doctor took an uncertain step and paused. "I seem to have lost my bearings, Kent. Would you give me your arm to the door?"

Joe followed blankly. It was the first time he had ever known his uncle to lose a sense of direction once established. Behind those blind eyes the room, in all its essentials, had been mapped. And even if its outlines had not been printed on a clear mind, the man had only to say,

"Lady, out!" and the dog would have taken him to the door. Why take Harley Kent's arm?

Captain Tucker, on the porch, spoke a greeting and passed inside. The door closed. Down at the end of the gravel where the driveway met the road, Joe instinctively turned toward home. But Dr.

Stone said, "Lady, right!" and was off toward the village at that amazingly rapid pace.

"I'm after pipe tobacco, Joe."

The boy's shorter legs beat a rapid tattoo on the dirt road. "I bought you some yesterday, Uncle David."

"An extra tin won't

go to waste," the man said casually.

Hedge and brush were full of fascinating odors that invited sniffing examination. But the shepherd dog, as though aware that the man who gripped the handle was in her keeping, went ahead with single-minded purpose. The dirt road became a paved street and they were in the town. Lady guided her charge toward the sidewalk, came to a cautious halt at the curb and waited for her command.

A voice called: "Dr. Stone! Dr. Stone!"

Joe saw that it was Tom Bloodgood, the jeweler. They waited, and Lady sat down on her haunches, watchful and alert.

"Heard about the robbery out your way, Doctor?"

"Yes."

"That's something I'd never expect to happen. I can't understand how a burglar could have got across that room without waking the dead. The way that floor creaked——"

"Kent says the storm

drowned all other noise." The doctor's mouth had grown hard at the corners. "I didn't know you and Kent were on visiting terms."

"We're not."

"But if you knew about those floor boards——"

"Oh! That was a business call—the only time I was in the

house. He sent for me last Wednesday——"

The voice stopped, and Joe found the jeweler's eyes resting on him meaningly. Flushing, the boy took himself out of earshot and pretended to be absorbed in a store window. Presently his uncle called to him, and they went down the street to Stevenson's shop, and Joe saw that the tight lines around the man's mouth had showed much deeper.

Back on the street the blind man was silent, and walked with quick steps beside the dog. Half way home a cloud of dust rode toward them, and Captain Tucker's car came out of the dust. The car stopped.

"So you didn't arrest Donovan," said the doctor.

The police officer leaned across the wheel. "Joe must have told you he's not in the car."

"Nobody had to tell me," Dr. Stone said mildly. "Captain Tucker, with a jewel thief in charge, would not be likely to stop for a chat with a friend. You didn't arrest Donovan?"

"N—no. Even though you're reasonably sure a man's guilty, you can't arrest him for robbery unless you have at least some proof. There is no proof—there's nothing. And he has an alibi. He and the maid have their rooms in the same wing of the house.

She says she couldn't sleep last night, and sat up and read with her door partly open. She insists Donovan couldn't pass that door without being seen or heard. If the maid's telling the truth, Donovan couldn't be the thief; if she isn't telling the truth, they're both in it. Anyway, if we do arrest Donovan, what about the necklace? If possible we want to recover that."

"But you think Donovan did it?"

"Well, Doctor, let's give it a look. She admits she never sat up all night reading before. She can't recollect ever leaving her door open before. Now, why did both those things have to happen last night when the safe was robbed?"

"It sounds rather convenient," Dr. Stone said.

"Too convenient. Too perfect. My idea is that Donovan did the job and the maid is hiding him. I can figure it all out, but I can't pin it on them. That girl's too slick for me. I'm going to call in State troopers. Maybe they'll be able to break down her story."

The car was gone with a whine of gears, and Joe stretched his legs and followed his uncle and the dog. Harley Kent's car stood in the driveway.

"We're at the Kent place, Uncle David."

"I know."

"Are we going in?"

"Sometimes," the doctor said cryptically, "it is best to leave a plum hang until it falls." The cane made a brisk gesture. "Tonight, Joe."

To the boy the night was a long way off. A crime had been committed in the neighborhood, almost under their noses, and the scene of the crime drew him with an excited, morbid curiosity. Late in the afternoon he walked back to the Kent place and loitered outside the hedge. He was there when a car drove in and two State troopers got out. Lean and trim in their belted uniforms, they looked competent and formidable; and his eyes, fascinated, clung to the bulges at their hips. An hour later they came out of the house, and Donovan was with them. The chauffeur was still with them when the car rolled away.

Joe ran for home. "Uncle David! They've arrested Donovan."

"Tucker?"

"No; State troopers.

I saw them take him away."

"I expected it," Dr. Stone said mildly. Joe, watching him, was presently aware that he slept peacefully in the depths of the porch chair. So can the blind, shut out from the light of the world, in turn shut out the world and drop off into almost instant slumber.

But at supper time the man was vividly awake. The strong, supple hands that had made him a surgeon, were suddenly restless and nervous.

"Joe," he said, "change those hard leather shoes to soft sneakers. Leather soles make too much noise."

The order had a sound of mystery and

adventure. Joe raced
upstairs to his room.
When he came down
the day was gone
and darkness lay
over the countryside.
Lady was already
harnessed. Out in the
road the boy held to
his uncle's arm and
hurried along. Here,
walking into a wall
of night, he would
by himself have to
go slowly. But to
his uncle the night

presented no change, nor did it bring up any new handicap. For to Dr. Stone the world was always dark and black. There was no day or night.

Kent's car was gone from the driveway. Dr. Stone said: "Easy, Joe; walk on the grass. Any lights?"

"Only in the back."

It seemed to the boy

that his uncle made a sound of satisfaction. The dog, as though sensing the man's desire for caution, led them slowly, silently. Dr. Stone's cane touched the tree.

"Lady!" His voice was low.

The dog was all attention.

"Lady, search. Fetch."

Joe was conscious of

the black bulk of the house, a black tower that was the tree, and a blurred shadow moving noiselessly in the grass. Minutes passed, and his heart pounded in his chest. One moment the dog was near him, and the next it was gone. And then the shadow stood motionless beside his uncle.

"Lady, again," Dr.

Stone urged. "Search. Fetch."

For what? Joe racked his brain and tried to find an answer. Once he heard the soft sniff of the dog, but could not see it. Suddenly it was beside his uncle again, motionless as before. How long it had been there he did not know.

"We'll go to the

house now," Dr. Stone said.

They crossed to the porch and rang the bell. The living room was all at once alight, and Harley Kent opened the door.

"I thought you might be along, Doctor. Come in; come in. It looks as though we've cleared this thing up."

"Then the necklace

was recovered?" Dr. Stone asked.

"No—not exactly. They'll sweat Donovan and make him come through. They took him away this afternoon."

"So I heard," the doctor said without emotion. "Under arrest?"

"Technically, no. They took him down

for questioning, but—
you know how those
things are worked.
Keep after him until
he opens up and then
book him. The maid
slipped."

"The maid?"

"Yes. They dragged
it out of her a little
at a time. Donovan
wanted her to marry
him. Yesterday he
urged her to marry
him and leave for the

West at once. That sounded suspicious, Doctor. With so many now out of work, why should a man marry and at once throw up his job? To do this he'd have to have quite a bit of money—and Donovan didn't have any. Or else he'd have to know how he could raise money very quickly. Get it?"

"Perfectly."

"So we sent out the maid and brought in Donovan. He had a smug answer to the reason for that trip to the West. A friend owned a taxi company in a western city and wanted him to come on and take the job of manager."

"He had this friend's letter, of course?"

Harley Kent laughed. "You're not as easily fooled as that, Doctor? Of course not. Said he had lost it. So the troopers took him away."

"That's that," Dr. Stone said after a silence.

"Exactly. And a lucky thing the girl talked. Up to that point we had nothing. No finger prints, no sign as to how the window had been forced, no sign of the necklace. Nothing but an open window and an open safe. It was as though a bird had flown in and had flown off with the jewels."

"A bird," Dr. Stone said slowly, and tapped his cane against the floor. "Nobody thought of that seriously though?"

"A bird?" Harley Kent stared.

To Joe's amazement, his uncle appeared in earnest. "Because if they had taken a bird seriously the next step——"

"The next step what?" Harley Kent demanded sharply.

The cane had ceased to tap the floor. "The

next step," Dr. Stone said softly, "would be to look where a bird would naturally fly with such a bauble."

Something electric, something unsaid, hung in the air, and Joe shook with a strange chill. Whatever that something was, it spoke to Lady. The dog grew restless and growled in its throat.

"I think we'll be going, Kent," said the doctor.

"Good night," said Harley Kent.

Joe clung to his uncle's arm and swallowed with difficulty. A hundred feet down the road the man halted.

"Can you see the house from here?"

"Yes, sir."

"Tell me when the downstairs lights go out." The man found his pipe and struck a match to the bowl.

A whippoorwill called musically through the night, and distance softened the hoot of an owl. Frogs croaked in a meadow and a rabbit stirred in the brush. Joe shifted from foot to foot, and wondered what was to come next. Twice cars passed them going into town, and off over the hill a dog howled. And then, without warning, the oblongs of downstairs windows disappeared and the roof was a dark patch against the sky.

"The lights are out," the boy whispered.

Dr. Stone put away the pipe. "Joe, you'd

better run home."

The boy had not expected this. "But——"

"Sorry, Joe. I can handle this better alone. You might only be in the way. Run along, and I'll tell you all about it in the morning."

"But if——"

"No ifs. Lady's here, and I'll be perfectly

all right. Off, now."

Without another word the boy trudged away. Once he looked back, and could just distinguish his uncle's form. Again he looked back, and man and dog were gone. His steps slowed and ceased. He stood listening.

The whippoorwill had ceased to call, and only the chorus

of frogs broke the stillness of the night. By and by he moved again, back the way he had come. The sneaks made his progress almost soundless. Had Uncle David told him to wear them so that they could go unnoticed to the pine tree? Why the tree?

Man and dog were gone from where he

had left them. The tree lingered in his mind. Avoiding the driveway he crept across the grass. A dark pillar, darker than the night, loomed ahead. It was the tree. He dropped to the ground and, hugging his knees, sat there and was almost afraid to breathe.

There was no moon, and the gloom was

filled with subtle alarms. Donovan was probably in a cell, caged and helpless. What would happen to the maid? And why that intangible something that had hung between Uncle David and Harley Kent? He grew cramped and shifted his position. It must be late. Where was his uncle? He strained his eyes toward the tree but could see nothing.

Suddenly every faculty was sharpened and drawn tight. He thought he had heard a sound. Slowly he relaxed. It must have been the wind. And then he heard it again. This time there could be no mistake. There had been a subdued, almost indistinct scraping.

Silence again, and darkness, and that vague alarm. The silence grew painful. A leaf, fluttering down, touched his face and a chill ran through his bones. Why should a leaf fall from a tree in early spring? And then the stillness was broken by a ringing call:

"Kent, it's no go."

A voice strangled and

strained, came down out of the tree. "Who the devil are you?"

"Dr. Stone. You can't get away with it, Kent. Tell them any story you like, but be sure you have Donovan released at once. Lady, home!"

Man and dog emerged out of the night, and Joe flattened out and hugged the ground.

"Come along, Joe," the doctor said.

The boy stood up, abashed, and took his uncle's arm. "How did you know I was there?"

"Ears—a blind man's ears. When you came in Lady remained quiet. That meant she recognized someone she trusted. There could be only one answer—you.

Do you realize you might have ruined everything? That's why I sent you home. One suspicious sound from outside the house and our quarry might have taken alarm."

Joe wet his lips. "It was Mr. Kent?"

"Of course. Donovan? I had my doubts from the start. Kent told a smooth story. He had had to give Donovan the combination, and the safe had been opened by combination. It was a tall man's safe, and Donovan was a tall man. It fitted together perfectly, Joe—too perfectly. Remember when I asked Kent to lead me to the door? I wanted to learn something—and I learned it. Kent is a tall man, too. I might have asked you, but to a boy all men seem tall."

"The maid's story was perfect, too," Joe said hesitatingly.

"Two perfect stories," Dr. Stone agreed. "It became a matter of picking the true from the false, and Kent rang false from the start."

"I don't understand,

Uncle David."

"Let's analyze it. When Kent came to the house Lady sneezed and drew away. Two weeks ago I upset a bottle of bay rum; it ran into her eyes and nose. She's been shy of bay rum since. When Kent said he'd lost his lighter and asked for a match he reeked with bay rum and talcum. The maid had awakened him at six o'clock, and he reached our house at eight. Two striking facts, Joe. Does a man, finding his house robbed in the night, calmly go upstairs and make a careful toilet? Does he wait two hours before going to a telephone to call the police?

"Well, we went

to his place. He wasn't home, and we wandered about the grounds. That was pure luck. We found the wet suit. I asked you if there was a pine tree on the place."

"Why, Uncle David?"

"Because that suit reeked with pine. We found that the tree was only six feet from the house and heavy-branched, which meant that some of the branches grew close to the house. And so now we had a robbery in the rain, a pine tree, and a dripping suit of Harley Kent's that reeked with pine. The facts were all unrelated, but I began to wonder if the tree had played a part in the robbery.

"Then Kent came back, and his first thought was to look in the wet suit for the missing lighter. When I mentioned the suit on the line he said nothing to indicate alarm. But a blind man's ears are sharp. They are quick to catch shades of sound in a voice. I knew he was disturbed because we had chanced upon that suit. Now, why should he be upset? Wet clothing is not uncommon after a wild rainstorm.

"We went to town for tobacco, and ran into Tom Bloodgood. That was another stroke of luck. For Bloodgood told me Kent had called him to the house to value a necklace. The jewelry market has fallen this last year, and Tom gave Kent a valuation of about $15,000. The moment Bloodgood told me that I thought I saw the picture.

"Kent's a market speculator. Evidently he had been hit and needed money. Apparently he didn't want to have the necklace appraised in New York where he was fairly well known—such things leak out and sometimes affect a man's credit. After he learned what the necklace would bring in the market he must have done some thinking. If he sold it, he'd realize $15,000. If it were stolen he'd collect $25,000 from the insurance company. The reason he had shaved and waited two hours to call the police took on significance. It began to look as though Kent had staged a convenient robbery. Collect for the jewels and still have them. Later he might break up the necklace and sell the pearls separately. It's been done before."

"Why didn't you tell Captain Tucker, Uncle David?"

"Oh, no. Tucker would have immediately searched the tree, and Kent could have got the incriminating suit out of the way and made the charge that Donovan had hidden the necklace in the pine. There was only one way. Scare Kent. Send him out into the tree in a panic. And then catch him in the act.

"So tonight we called upon Kent. I was searching for a way to alarm him, and he opened the door himself by mentioning birds. The moment I spoke of a search of a tree he froze. After that it was merely a matter of waiting for him to come forth to remove the proof of his guilt."

They were almost

at Joe's house. The boy turned a puzzled thought in his mind.

"But, Uncle David——"

"Yes."

"Even if there was pine on his coat it wouldn't be proof he'd been in a pine tree."

"True," Dr. Stone agreed. "That's what sent me searching for the absolute proof."

Light broke upon the boy. "I see it now. You found something?"

"This." The man held out his hand.

In the darkness the boy could not see what lay in the hand. "What is it, Uncle David?"

"The missing cigar lighter," Dr. Stone said quietly. "It fell out of Kent's pocket while he was hiding the jewels. Lady found it for me under the tree."

THE END

ABOUT THE AUTHOR

William Heylinger was a prolific author of books for readers of all ages. He wrote baseball stories in " The St. Mary's Series." His blind detective, Dr. David Stone has provided joy and inspiration to many. He died in 1955.

ABOUT THE COVER

The image on the cover is adapted from a poster for an Italian raincoat called the Impermeabili Moretti. Leopoldo Meticovitz is the artist.

WHAT WE'RE ABOUT

I started making Super Large Print books for my grandma. I wanted books that she could keep reading as her glaucoma and macular degeneration advanced. So I chose a font originally designed for people with dyslexia, because the letters are bold and easy to distinguish. It is set at

30 pt, nearly twice the size of traditional Large Print books.

Digital reading was too frustrating for my grandma. It could never offer the pleasures she had always associated with reading: the peacefulness of turning a page, the satisfaction in knowing a story has "this much left," and the comforting memories of adventure, companionship, and revelation she felt when seeing the cover of her favorite book. Part of what makes reading so relaxing and grounding is the tactile experience. I hope these books can bring joy to those who want to keep reading and to those who've never had the pleasure of curling up with a page turner.

Please let me know if these books are helpful to you and if you have any requests for new titles. To leave feedback and to see the complete and constantly updating catalog, please visit:

superlargeprint.com

MORE BOOKS AT:

superlargeprint.com

KEEP ON READING!

ISBN 978-1719585569
ISBN 1719585563

Made in the USA
Monee, IL
17 October 2021